BAYOU SONG

To my husband, Jeff,
who makes living on the bayou a daily adventure.
–Margaret Simon

To the loving people in my life who always support my creating.
–Anna Cantrell

ISBN 13 (paper): 978-1-946160-23-2

http://ulpress.org
University of Louisiana at Lafayette Press
P.O. Box 43558
Lafayette, LA 70504-3558

Printed on acid-free paper in Canada
Library of Congress Cataloging-in-Publication Data

Names: Simon, Margaret Gibson, author. | Cancienne, Henry, 1946- photographer. | Cantrell, Anna, illustrator.
Title: Bayou song / poetry by Margaret Simon ; photography by Henry Cancienne ; illustrations by Anna Cantrell.
Description: Lafayette, LA : University of Louisiana at Lafayette Press, 2018.
Identifiers: LCCN 2018006652 | ISBN 9781946160232 (acid-free paper)
Subjects: LCSH: Children's poetry, American.
Classification: LCC PS3619.I5624 A6 2018 | DDC 811/.6--dc23
LC record available at https://lccn.loc.gov/2018006652

Bayou Song

Creative Explorations of the South Louisiana Landscape

Poetry by Margaret Simon
Photography by Henry Cancienne
Illustrations by Anna Cantrell

2018
University of Louisiana at Lafayette Press

Legend of Bayou Teche

Long ago, in the days when Native American tribes lived in harmony with the land, there lived a huge venomous snake. The snake's body stretched for miles and miles. The Chitimacha tribe warriors gathered together to conquer this enemy snake. To kill a hundred-mile-long snake was no easy task, so it took days for the snake to die. As the snake fought to survive, it twisted and turned and created a great gorge in the soil, eventually dying and decomposing, leaving behind Bayou Teche.

I am a Beckoning Brown Bayou

I am a beckoning brown bayou.
I wonder where my water runs.
I echo egret, heron, and ibis.
I watch waving leaves of cypress trees.
I call your name.

I am a beckoning brown bayou.
I twist and turn like a water snake.
I touch fur and scales and fins.
I nurture nutria, raccoons, and gators.
I want you to come in.

I am a beckoning brown bayou.
I remember tales of Acadians and explorers.
I say courage lives here.
I reveal my secrets at twilight.
I hope you'll stay awhile.

Write it: Choose a place in nature (an ocean, a tree, a flower, an animal) to write about. If you use personification (as in "I am a Beckoning Brown Bayou"), you become the thing you are writing about. How would an ocean, tree, flower, or animal feel, act, hear, smell, or see?

SKETCH IT: What is a waterway near you? Does it have a shape? Does the shape match its name? Draw the waterway so that it matches its name.

Spanish Moss

Spanish moss is not moss at all. It is a type of bromeliad, like a pineapple, believe it or not. Spanish moss grows in areas of Mexico, South America, the southern United States, and the Caribbean.

This hanging hair-like plant was named Spanish moss by the French who thought the plant resembled the beards of the Spanish conquistadors.

Spanish moss does not root or use the host tree for nutrients. Nutrients come from rain, sunlight, and dust.

The early Acadians who settled in South Louisiana used Spanish moss mixed with mud for mortar on their houses. This mixture of mud and moss is called bousillage (pronounced boo-see-ahj).

Bayou Fairy Tale

Spanish moss twirls
Like Rapunzel's hair curls
In ghostly gray swirls.

Write it: "Bayou Fairy Tale" is a tercet, a poem of three lines. Think of something in nature that reminds you of something else. How is a tree like a soldier, for example? How is a vine like a snake? Write a three-lined poem. You may choose to rhyme, but it is not necessary in a tercet.

Sketch it: Draw an imaginary character with something from nature for hair: moss, grass, leaves, anything you can think of.

Eagles

Bald eagles are a regal, yet rare, sight in South Louisiana. They were harmed by toxic DDT, a chemical once used to kill mosquitoes and other pests, but have recently made a strong comeback from near extinction. Eagles live near water because they are avid fishers. They make nests high in cypress trees using sticks and moss. Eagles lay their eggs in November and stay with the nest until the baby eaglets can fly in the summer.

Duckweed

Made up of clusters of small floating fronds, duckweed covers the surface of quiet, still water. As its name suggests, many breeds of ducks eat duckweed. The plant can spread so thick that it looks like a grassy field rather than the watery surface of a bayou.

Duckweed is both good and bad for the environment. If duckweed gets too thick and out of control, it can take oxygen from the water, killing fish. But duckweed also prevents the spread of mosquitoes and algae growth.

There is Always

There is always
a light
flowing through leaves
creating stained glass
on a duckweed carpet.

There is always
an altar
emerging as a pyramid,
fans of needles pray
in the sanctuary.

There is always
a cathedral
rising near the bayou
where bald eagles nest
in a bell tower.

WRITE IT: Think of *your* favorite place in nature. What is always there for you? Write a poem using the repeated line, "There is always…"

SKETCH IT: Draw the very top of a tall tree. What kind of nest would you build? Fill the tree with your nest.

Great Blue Heron

With his head tucked into his shoulders, the great blue heron flies close to the surface of the water using strong, slow wing beats. A stealthy solo fisher, this bird stands silently near the bayou, waiting and watching. The great blue heron has a varied diet of mostly fish, but also frogs, turtles, snakes, insects, and rodents. The song of the heron is not melodic or sweet. He announces his take-off or landing with loud croaks. The heron is a beauty to behold.

Louisiana Bayou Song*

Sometimes on the bayou in Louisiana
a storm rolls in quickly—
Cypress trees
sway to the sound.

Sometimes on a quiet day
when the sun is high and hot
a heron happens by—
The bayou slows to the beat of his wading.

The song of the bayou
can be as fast and frenetic as a Zydeco two-step
or as soft and slow as a Cajun waltz—
The bayou sings a song to me.

* To be published in *The Poetry of US: More than 200 Poems that Celebrate the People, Places, and Passions of the United States*, ed. J. Patrick Lewis (National Geographic Children's Books, 2018).

Write it: Sometimes writers use anthropomorphism by making an animal do things a person would do, such as birds dancing or a raccoon playing a violin. Choose an animal. Imagine the animal doing something you do and write a story or poem about it.

SKETCH IT: What is your favorite musical instrument? Draw a picture of the instrument being played by an animal. You may use your sketch to inspire your writing.

Alligators

The American alligator is one of the largest reptiles roaming the earth today. Louisiana and Florida have the highest populations of alligators in the United States, but you will have to travel near marshland to find them. Alligators are cold-blooded, so they often sun themselves on banks or logs floating in the water. They are inactive during the winter months. Female alligators build their nests of marsh grasses by pulling this thick vegetation into a mound. She creates a hole, lays twenty to thirty eggs, and covers the cavity with more vegetation in order to incubate the eggs. The female gator stays close to the nest and will aggressively guard it from predators. When the eggs are ready to hatch, they let out a squeal and momma alligator uncovers the nest. The babies will stay close to their mother for a year, sometimes longer.

Gator Picnic

We count the gators one by one.
They've all come out to chase the sun.

Leather-black armor, ridgy and rough,
Razor sharp teeth, spiky and tough,

A gathering of clumsy beasts
Accustomed to carnivorous feasts.

Mouths agape keep them cool;
Watch out for their monstrous drool!

A gator picnic shouldn't be attended
by anyone who would be offended.

Count the gators in the sun.
What's for lunch? Are you the one?

WRITE IT: "Alligator Picnic" uses rhyming couplets. A couplet is two rhyming lines of similar length. Write a rhyming couplet about a baby alligator.

Sketch it: What kind of picnic do you like? Do you sit on the ground on a blanket or at a picnic table? Do you have all your favorite foods or is it an elaborate feast or just a few snacks? Design a drawing of your best picnic ever.

Crawfish
(also called crayfish)

This small crustacean that is related to the lobster is a huge part of Cajun culture in Louisiana. On a spring day, residents fire up their crawfish pots and have a crawfish boil, a party for eating pounds of crawfish. Usually only the tail is eaten, but some natives will suck the fat from the head. Crawfish is the number one export from Louisiana to restaurants all over the world.

Crawfish live in the muddy waters of bayous and swamps. In the fall and winter, they burrow underground in water-filled tunnels. Near the bayou, you can see crawfish chimneys, a mound of mud pellets that looks like a smokestack. Most commercial crawfish, however, are raised in ponds and captured in wire nets shaped like funnels.

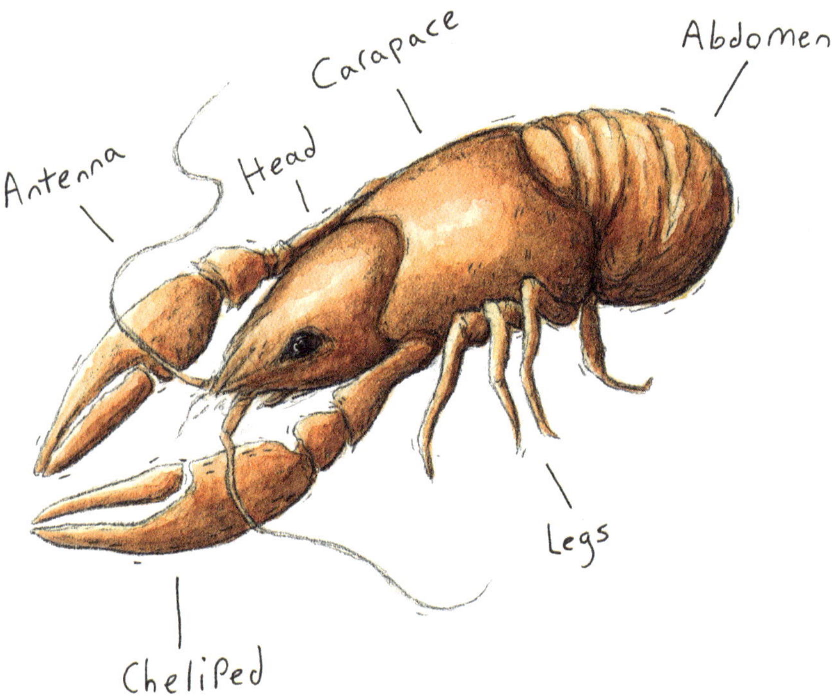
Carapace
Abdomen
Antenna
Head
Legs
Cheliped

The Geometry of Crawfish

Grab a long line antenna
Avoid looking into round peppercorn peepers
Hold the cylinder cavity containing fat
Watch out for triangular tweezer pincers
Detach the arced accordion tail
Remove curvy meaty muscle
Dip in a puddle-circle of spicy ketchup
Eat

WRITE IT: Make a list of geometry words—words about shapes. Choose an animal to describe using shapes. What shape is a snake or a bird's beak? What about a cat's nose?

Sketch it: Draw a picture of an animal. Label its parts.

Bald Cypress Trees

The bald cypress trees shed needles in the fall. This is why "bald" is part of its name. They can grow very tall and especially like to grow near wet, swampy land. These protector trees prevent erosion by holding the soil close with their roots, keeping it from washing away.

Bald cypress produce cones. Their cones are round and green at first and then become woody.

Bald cypress trees live a long time, sometimes up to six hundred years. They can be breeding grounds for amphibians and catfish. Wood ducks nest in the hollow and bald eagles nest high in the tree canopy.

Bald Cypress "Knees"

The Bald Cypress grows as a buttressed tree with a wide base. The knees may serve as more stability for the root system which grows just below the surface. Early scientists believed the knees help to deliver oxygen from the air to the roots, but this theory has not been proven.

Cypress Zeno

They stick up like a woody weed
grounding cypress
roots that
hold
sculpted figures
growing
bold.
Not really knees
so I'm
told.

Write it: Try a zeno poem. A zeno is a poetry form created by J. Patrick Lewis, U.S. Children's Poet Laureate 2011-2013. This form was inspired by the mathematical hailstone sequence which always ends in 4-2-1. A zeno is a ten-lined poem with the syllable count of 8, 4, 2, 1, 4, 2, 1, 4, 2, 1 in which the one-syllable lines rhyme.

Sketch it: What other things in nature have "knees?" Draw a bird, animal, or other plant form that is like our cypress trees with knees.

Nutria
(also called coypu)

Agile and comfortable in the water, nutria are large web-footed rodents. Nutria eat a variety of marsh vegetation and small aquatic creatures like snails and mussels. Once found only in South America, they were bred for their warm fur undercoat. The population of nutria has become invasive in South Louisiana so that hunters are paid a small price for a nutria pelt.

Nutria Blues

Nutria, Nutria

New
        tree
                uh!

You invaded our fragile wetlands.

With your bright orange tusks
and your whip-like tail,
you look like an overgrown rat!

Nutria, Nutria

New
        tree
                uh!

South American soldier cadet,

with your grand appetite
for all things green,
Watch out! You're going to get fat!

Nutria, Nutria

New
        tree
                uh!

A bounty on your pelt.

With shaggy brown fur,
and a soft undergrowth,
you're likely to be made into a hat.

Write it: "Nutria Blues" is a poem of address. The writer speaks directly to the topic as if they are having a conversation. What animal would you like to have a conversation with? Write a poem of address.

SKETCH IT: Artists and illustrators put clothing on animals to make them seem more like humans. What animal could you put clothes on? Draw an animal with a piece of clothing on.

Barred Owls

In the forest near the swamp, the barred owl's signature call "Who cooks for you?" echoes at dawn. They are nocturnal, which means they hunt at night for the small rodents they eat. Barred owls roost silently during the day, nesting most often in tree cavities.

Barred Owl

Mr. Owl hoots a call,
Who cooks for you all?

Soulful eyes
From hollow spies

Moon rises
Forest disguises

Shadows dance
Bayou's trance

Marking mole,
mouse, or vole—

Barred wings hover
Strong talons cover

Noiseless flight
Deep dark night

Write it: This poem is made up of mostly two to three-word phrases that describe a barred owl. What is a bird you know well? Make a list of words to describe the bird. Your list can become a poem.

Sketch it: The face of an owl is unique and recognizable. Draw an owl's face. Follow the line from the nose around the two eyes. An owl can see in the dark because he has a large dark pupil. Make the owl's pupil large with another larger circle around it.

Raccoons

Raccoons can be found almost anywhere in North America. They thrive in forests, but also have adapted quite well to life in cities because they will eat anything. Their dexterous hands can catch a fish in one swoop or pry open a garbage can lid. Raccoons hunt and forage at night. They may create a den in a hollow tree or the attic of a house. Raccoons typically hibernate in cold climates and have one to seven cubs in early summer.

Dear Mama Raccoon,

I think you've been quite mischievous
under the veil of night.
You've left a trail that's suspicious
of nocturnal delight.

I know you're not malicious
attracted by the smell,
but do you find that trash nutritious
to feed your kittens well?

I hope you will forgive us
for locking up the bin.
We're weary of your surreptitious
ways of getting in.

This may be too ambitious—
I've left a different trail.
So please be more judicious
and take my mother's kale!

WRITE IT: The poem is a letter poem to the mother raccoon. What animal could you write a letter to? You can use a rhyming pattern if you want.

SKETCH IT: Draw a raccoon starting with a rounded half-circle for a head. Draw a round nose at the base of the half-circle. Draw two small eyes on either side of the nose. For the mask, draw a half-oval around each eye. Add details of ears and whiskers.

Resurrection Fern

While most plants can only lose 10 percent of their water content without dying, a resurrection fern loses up to 97 percent, reducing the fronds to greyish brown clumps, and rises back to full bright green once the rain comes. The fern is aptly named because resurrection means to come back to life. The fern, however, does not die; it just looks dead. This fern needs a host plant to live on, usually a large oak, but it doesn't take any of the tree's nutrients. Because of this, a resurrection fern can continue to live on a fallen branch.

Resurrection Fern

Brown fronds,
sheltered by mother tree limbs,
        wake up
                green
                        after rain.

No longer curled and dry,
paper-lace fragments of butterfly wings—
        unfurl
                spring.

WRITE IT: "Paper-laced fragments of butterfly wings" is a metaphor. A metaphor is a figure of speech comparing two subjects that are not alike but have similar characteristics. To create a metaphor, try this exercise: Take an object from nature and call it something different but similar: A leaf is a swirling scarf in the wind. Collect metaphors in your notebook to use in your writing.

Sketch it: Find an object in nature and study it carefully. Without looking at your paper, try to draw the object following the lines of the object with your eyes. This is called contour drawing, an outline drawing. You are training your eyes to see the shapes of things.

Great White Egret

Tall and skinny with a signature long curved neck, the great white egret is a quiet wading hunter. Scouting for small fish, frogs, or other water tidbits, the great white egret will strike its prey with amazing speed. All feathers on this bird are white making it a brilliant sight in the blue sky. These birds are colonial nesters, which means they often nest together in a grove of tall cypress trees jutting out of a bayou or swamp.

Peep-eye

I spy

daylight-christening
feather-glistening

wing-shaking
baby-waking

hungry-crying
Mama eyeing

worm-juggling
nest-snuggling

Hello, morning
Great egret

WRITE IT: Word play is fun. In the "Peep-Eye" poem, the ending -ing was added to verbs to make them into a new form of adjective. Think about some action words you could change to adjectives. How would you describe yourself? Are you fun-loving? soccer ball-juggling? chocolate-craving?

Sketch it: Do you remember playing Peep-Eye? Did you hold your hands up over your eyes? Did you hide behind a table or door? Hold your hands over your eyes and "peep" through your fingers. Think about how what you see while "peeping" is a little different than when you aren't. Draw what you see.

Wisteria

Wisteria is a flowering vine that grows very quickly and will take over a fence post, the trunk of a tree, or anything it can climb on. The falling clusters of flowers bloom in spring and are full of fragrance, attracting numerous bees.

Weeping Wisteria

Lavender locks spill from the sky.
In bloom, wisteria curls cry.
Sweet nectar tears fall.
Purple peapods sprawl.
Bright bees crawl,
lick them dry.

Write it: The poem, "Weeping Wisteria," is a Welsh poetry form called a clogyrnach:

Line 1: 8 syllables with an a rhyme
Line 2: 8 syllables with an a rhyme
Line 3: 5 syllables with a b rhyme
Line 4: 5 syllables with a b rhyme
Line 5: 3 syllables with a b rhyme
Line 6: 3 syllables with an a rhyme

Forms can be challenging, but can also give you a creative way to write a message. Using an online rhyme site can help you find rhyming words to try.

SKETCH IT: Think about the wisteria from the bee's point of view. Is it a candy store? cafeteria? or snack bar? Draw the wisteria from the bee's perspective.

White Ibis

The white ibis is identified by its long reddish pink curved bill and long wading red legs. These striking birds flock together for nesting and hunting. They can drag their bill through the mud to find insects and crawfish. The white ibis can be found near wetland areas of the southern United States and the Caribbean.

White Ibis Triptych

I.
It's in the way
white ibis water-wades
on shallow shadows.

II.
It's the way black wingtips
wave through a cloud-glide
to cypress tops.

III.
It's the beat of a curved tweezer-bill
insect-probing
in marshy grass.

WRITE IT: A triptych is a work of art in three parts. Think about three ways an animal moves. Write three lines in three stanzas to create your own triptych.

SKETCH IT: The body of a white ibis is shaped like a feathery football. To draw the head and beak, create a long curved line the length of your pointer finger. Add long legs with three toes.

Toads

The Gulf Coast toad is a common toad living in the southern part of the United States. They live on dry land but are also found near marshes and swamps. They are active during the spring and summer. On warm summer nights, the males blow their bellow-like jaws to make a loud mating call.

Ode to a Toad

You blow
your bassoon
by ballooning
your throat,
slow release
filling twilight
with sound.
A song
only she-toad will love,
echoing along the bayou.
I hear creepy calls
rising, falling
like the breath
of a resting bear
snoring,
mooring,
daring
me to sleep.

Write it: An ode is a poem of praise addressed to a specific object. Pablo Neruda, a Chilean poet (1904–1973), made the ode famous when he wrote multiple odes to common things like "Ode to my Socks" and "Ode to the Book." His odes had few words in each line and are written in free verse (no rhyme or meter). Fold your page in half: using only half the page, write an ode to a common object that has meaning in your life.

SKETCH IT: Draw a picture of the object or animal you wrote your ode for.

Black-Crowned Night-Heron

Short and stocky, the black-crowned night-heron is smaller than its cousin, the great blue heron. These birds forage in the wetlands at dusk or at night. They eat small salt-water and marsh creatures, including crawfish, worms, and insects, as well as plant material. They scoop their prey into their bill rather than stabbing it like other herons.

What the Black-Crowned Night-Heron Knows

To fold his neck under his head,
and rest inside a cattail bed.
To hunt along the water's edge.
To wait for twilight to be fed.

This is what the night heron knows.

Be alert to the slightest splash—
crawfish, snake, or worms that thrash,
the slightest ripple, piece of trash
may end up in his beak's great cache.

This is what the night heron knows.

WRITE IT: "What the Black-Crowned Night-Heron Knows" is a Deeper Wisdom poem, a form created by poet Joyce Sidman. Once you select a topic, ask yourself what does this object know. State the deeper truths in two stanzas. You may rhyme each final word if you choose.

Sketch it: Many bayou birds wade in the shallow edges of the bayou hidden by cattails and other plants. Draw a bird wading in and around tall grasses. Can you hide the bird in the foliage?

Snapping Turtle

Snapping turtles are large turtles found only in North America. The largest freshwater turtle, the alligator snapping turtle can grow to over two hundred pounds. Snapping turtles lure their prey in with a worm-like appendage on the end of their tongues. The alligator snapping turtle has a longer neck and spikier shell than the common snapping turtle. Both spend most of their time under water. They do not like human contact and make terrible pets. Their snap can be a treacherous bite.

Things to do if you're a Snapping Turtle

Wear a grey-green coat;
Call it a carapace.
Pretend to be an alligator.
Camouflage yourself with mud.
Periscope your nose for some air.
Take out the trash from bayou's bottom.
Stick out your tongue to lure a minnow in.
Dig for a tasty crawfish.
Linger on a cypress root along the bayou's edge.
Bask in the afternoon sun seeping through the trees.
Never leave your room.

WRITE IT: A Things to Do poem is a type of list poem that can capture personification of an animal or object. Start with a list of things the animal or object can do using action words. For example, a butterfly can flutter, swoop, soar, find, and sip. Then add a phrase to your chosen verbs. Flutter to the brightest flower, for example. Create a Things to Do poem with your list.

Sketch it: If you have written a Things to Do poem, illustrate it with a sketch.

Southern Live Oak

The southern live oak is a majestic tree that symbolizes life in the South. These trees grow to be as tall as fifty feet and as wide as eighty feet. Their branches grow out and down sweeping toward the ground and back up again. Live oaks can live a very long life, up to four hundred years. They are nearly evergreen, which means that they drop and replace their leaves over a short period in spring. Many animals depend on the seed of a live oak (acorns), for survival through winter months.

The Live Oaks— Grow Unnoticed*

The Live Oaks—grow unnoticed—
Their Moss covered figures rise
Without effort—Collapse—
Comfort—or Celebration—

In Their Draping Arms
the Raccoon—with sheer impulse
climbs high—and hidden—masked—
finds home—at night—

*after Emily Dickinson's "The Mountains—Grow Unnoticed"

Write it: Poets and artists often copy famous works of art in order to learn and practice technique. This poem is based on a famous Emily Dickinson poem, "The Mountains—Grow Unnoticed." Find a poem that you like and create a matching poem by replacing words and phrases with your own.

Sketch it: Have you ever noticed how a tree grows? Imagine your hand following the tree as it grows. Draw a large tree, fill the page, sprawl the branches wide, and add clusters of leaves.

Bayou Teche

The Bayou Teche was once the Mississippi River. Over the course of thousands of years, the Mississippi River would flood and recede, dropping sediment—creating the Teche Ridge and the Bayou Teche. A bayou is a boggy and slow moving stream. Humans have attempted to control the flooding that is natural to this waterway. The human control and interaction with the bayou is important, but it also depletes the fertile nutrients and natural habitat of the ridge. Organizations such as The T.E.C.H.E. Project are working to restore some of this loss and damage.

Bayou Sunset Tanka

Mandarin sky melts
Into a bayou-soda pop
Orange spritz backdrop

Dancing moss-hair shadows
Skip along with ebb and flow.

WRITE IT: What words in this poem have a taste? Can you imagine the taste while reading the poem? Think of a flavor you love. Write a description of a place with flavor words.

SKETCH IT: Sunset has been inspiration for artists for at least as long as the Bayou Teche has flowed. Sketch a sunset in a place that you love.

Bayou Teche Waterway

More Resources

Mental Floss: mentalfloss.com

National Wildlife Federation: www.nwf.org

All About Birds: www.allaboutbirds.org

The T.E.C.H.E. Project: www.techeproject.org

Venerable Trees: venerabletrees.org

Barnes, Michelle Heidenrich. 2016, 2017. *The Best of Today's Little Ditty.* Gainesville, Florida: Igoo Island Press.

Heard, Georgia. 1999. *Awakening the Heart: Exploring Poetry in the Elementary and Middle School.* Portsmouth, New Hampshire: Heinemann.

Janeczko, Paul B. 1994. *Poetry from A to Z.* New York: Simon & Schuster Books for Young Readers.

Lyne, Sandford. 2007. *Writing Poetry from the Inside Out: Finding your Voice through the Craft of Poetry.* Naperville, Illinois: Sourcebooks.

Magliaro, Elaine. 2017. *Things to Do*. San Francisco, California: Chronicle Books.

Sidman, Joyce. 2014. *Winter Bees.* Boston, Massachusetts: Houghton Mifflin Harcourt Books for Young Readers.

VanDerwater, Amy Ludwig. 2017. *Poems are Teachers: How Studying Poetry Strengthens Writing in All Genres.* Portsmouth, New Hampshire: Heinemann.

Vardell, Sylvia and Wong, Janet. 2016. *You Just Wait: A Poetry Friday Power Book.* Princeton, New Jersey: Pomelo Books.

Vardell, Sylvia and Wong, Janet. 2017. *Here We Go: A Poetry Friday Power Book.* Princeton, New Jersey: Pomelo Books.

Wolf, Allan. 2006. *Immersed in Verse.* Asheville, North Carolina: Lark Books.

Acknowledgments

To UL Press associate director, James Wilson, and production manager, Mary Duhé, for trusting in my work enough to devote time and effort to making it happen and with careful consideration of young readers, artists, and writers.

To Anna Cantrell, for seeing clearly the animals and plants of the bayou with a creative eye. Your illustrations make my heart sing!

To Henry Cancienne, for freely giving amazing photographs that enhance our view into bayou living.

To Philip Gould, whose photograph of gators in UL's swamp inspired one of my first Bayou Song poems, "Gator Picnic," and for offering your professional photos for inclusion.

To my virtual writing group in multiple meetings by video conferencing, for gently leading me to my own discoveries: Catherine Flynn, Linda Mitchell, Heidi Mordhorst, and Julie Burchstead.

To my face-to-face writing group, supporting me for eighteen years through many writing journeys: Kay Couvillon, Dianne Dempsey-Legnon, and Marion Rosser.

To Irene Latham, for reading early drafts and pushing my writing and my confidence.

To Paul Schexnayder, for always being a text away to cheer me on.

To my husband, Jeff, for giving me love, for taking me canoeing, for caring for our space on the bayou, and for rescuing me from snakes.

To all of you, thanks for being instrumental in the creation of this exploration of my home, Bayou Teche.

About the Author

Margaret Simon is a Mississippi native who married into a Louisiana life. She lives on the Bayou Teche in New Iberia, Louisiana, with her husband, Jeff. Their now empty nest once housed three daughters, Maggie, Katherine, and Martha. Margaret has been an elementary school teacher for thirty-one years, most recently teaching gifted students in Iberia Parish. She has published poems in the journal *The Aurorean*, anthologies for *Today's Little Ditty*, in Poetry Friday Power Book *Here We Go*, and in National Geographic's the *Poetry of US*. Border Press published her collection of poems with her father's Christmas card art, *Illuminate* in fall of 2013. *Blessen*, a novel for young readers, was published in April 2012, also by Border Press. In her teaching profession, she has a Masters degree in Gifted Education and certification by the National Boards for Professional Teaching Standards. Margaret writes a blog regularly at www.reflectionsontheteche.com.

About the Illustrator

Anna Amelia Cantrell is a freelance illustrator based in south Louisiana. Her work is full of whimsical, nature filled watercolors of interesting animals, characters, plenty of trees, and other growing things. Anna spends her free time drinking lots of tea, looking after plants, taking mild adventures, and collecting things—from stories to moss and rocks. Visit her online at www.instagram.com/jarofpencils/

Praise for Bayou Song

"Any child who has this book has a source book, field guide, workbook, nature guide, and a wonderful set of poems that teach everything a beginning poet needs to know to write a first poem, and a second one, and a third one, and on and on. I love this book!"

–Darrell Bourque, Former Louisiana Poet Laureate

"Part field guide, part poetry collection, and part naturalist's notebook, this symphony of words, art, and images will leave readers spellbound by the beauty of the bayou. Inspiration abounds, and nature-lovers young and old will thrill at the opportunity to add their own poems and sketches to this celebration of South Louisiana's unique landscape."

–Irene Latham, poetry editor for *Birmingham Arts Journal* and author of *Leaving Gee's Bend*, 2011 ALLA Children's Book of the Year

"This is a generous, generative book that gives and gives and does not make demands. My fingers were itching to hold a pencil, a canoe paddle, a watercolor set, a camera. I leave its universe a little sad to go, but refreshed in my love of the Louisiana bayous and with my own creativity restored."

Ava Leavell Haymon, author of *Eldest Daughter: Poems* (LSU Press)
Poet Laureate, State of Louisiana, 2013-2015

"Margaret's poems drip with the sights, sounds, and textures of the bayou! Full of wonderful word choices and unexpected images, her poems are fun to read and easy to understand. . . . This book is an amazing resource for teachers in the bayou—or anyone who'd like to go on a mental bayou field trip!"

–Laura Purdie Salas, Author of more than 125 books for kids, including *Meet My Family!*, *If You Were the Moon*, *Water Can Be...*, and *BookSpeak!*